D0490217

631 0317
FLC 93/ 72259 6/94 JAB.
P reserve stock

Text copyright © 1993 by Jeanne Willis
Illustrations copyright © 1993 by Tony Ross

The rights of Jeanne Willis and Tony Ross to be identified as the author and illustrator of this work have
been asserted by them in accordance with the Copyright, Designs and Patents Act, 1988.

First published in Great Britain in 1993 by Andersen Press Ltd., 20 Vauxhall Bridge Road, London
SW1V 2SA. Published in Australia by Random House Australia Pty., 20 Alfred Street, Milsons Point,
Sydney, NSW 2061. All rights reserved. Colour separated in Switzerland by Photolitho AG,
Offsetreproduktionen, Gossau, Zurich. Printed and bound in Italy by Grafiche AZ, Verona.

10   9   8   7   6   5   4   3   2   1

British Library Cataloguing in Publication Data available.

ISBN 0 86264 403 8

This book has been printed on acid-free paper

DR XARGLE'S BOOK OF EARTH RELATIONS

Translated into Human by Jeanne Willis
Pictures by Tony Ross

Andersen Press · London

Good morning, class. Today we are going to learn about Earth Family.

An Earth Family is a collection of Earthlings who belong to each other whether they like it or not.

They are many different ages from brand new to antique.

They have identical earflaps and hooter shapes.

A family begins with a mummy Earthling and daddy Earthling and one Earthlet.

The number of relatives in an Earth Family is always larger than the number of chairs at Christmas time.

A family row begins with two Earthlets called Bother and Sulker.

Bother Earthlets are smelly, sticky and dangerous.
Never look in their pockets.

For supper they eat wiggly worms.

Sulker Earthlets are sly and sneaky and can be recognised by their piercing shrieks.

To make them do this drop a webby eight legs down their frillies.

They squirt many gallons of water from their two eyes.

Here are Aunty and Uncle Earthling. When they come to visit, the Earthlets must frisk them on the doorstep for expensive gifts.

The Uncle Earthling is forced to crawl about on all fours like a neddy.

Everybody has to play a game called "Be quiet. We are talking". The winner is the last one to fall asleep.

Here are some phrases I would like you to learn:
"Gosh, is that the time?"
"We really must be going."

These are Grandpa and Grandma Earthling. They were born on Planet Earth at the same time as Tyrannosaurus Rex.

They are made from soft, crumpled material.

The Grandma Earthling grows fruit and flowers on her head.

At night, she puts pink hedgehogs in her fur. The Grandpa Earthling puts his fangs in a glass.

Earthlets and ancient Earthlings behave in the same way. Here they all are at a bread-throwing competition. The winner is the one who hits the most ducks without falling in.

The most popular game is called "Where did I put my glasses?" This is something the whole family can enjoy.

That is the end of today's lesson. Put your disguises on
quickly. Matron has kindly arranged for us to meet a
real Earth family.

Have you all got your wedding invitations?

We will be landing at Buckingham Palace in five seconds.